FOX TALE

by YOSSI ABOLAFIA

 Greenwillow Books, New York

Watercolors and ink were used for the full-color art.
The text type is Bryn Mawr Book.
Copyright © 1991 by Yossi Abolafia
All rights reserved. No part of this book
may be reproduced or utilized in any form
or by any means, electronic or mechanical,
including photocopying, recording, or by
any information storage and retrieval
system, without permission in writing
from the Publisher, Greenwillow Books,
a division of William Morrow & Company, Inc.,
105 Madison Avenue, New York, NY 10016.
Printed in Singapore by Tien Wah Press
First Edition 10 9 8 7 6 5 4 3 2 1

Library of Congress Cataloging-in-Publication Data
Abolafia, Yossi.
Fox tale / by Yossi Abolafia.
p.   cm.
Summary: Donkey, Crow, and Rabbit join
forces to prevent Fox from swindling Bear
out of a jar of honey.
ISBN 0-688-09541-0. ISBN 0-688-09542-9 (lib. bdg.)
[1. Foxes—Fiction.   2. Animals—Fiction.
3. Swindlers and swindling—Fiction.]
I. Title   PZ7.A165Fo   1991
[E]—dc20   89-77501   CIP   AC

FOR ITAMAR

Bear was strolling happily in the woods,
licking honey out of a jar.
Two greedy eyes were watching him from
behind a bush.

"Hi, Stumpy!" called Fox.

"What did you call me?" asked Bear.

"Stumpy," said Fox. "That's what everybody calls you behind your back."

"They do?" said Bear.

"All the time," said Fox. "Because you have no tail."

"I have a tail," said Bear.
"Everybody else has a better one than you,"
 said Fox. "But you can have a good one, too."
"Really?" said Bear.
"I'll trade you my beautiful bushy tail for
 your half-empty jar of honey," said Fox.

"But how can I take your tail with me?" asked Bear.

"You don't have to. I'll keep it for you," said Fox.

"As you can see, I've always taken excellent care of it."

"But how will anyone know it's mine?" asked Bear.

"I'll hang a sign on it," said Fox.

"What if you're not around?" asked Bear.

"I'll give you a note," said Fox. "A guarantee—or your honey back."

Meanwhile, down by the stream, some animals were having their afternoon tea. They were busily discussing the cunning Fox.

"I was sitting on a branch eating my lunch one day," said Crow. "Fox stopped by and said, 'A charming bird like you must have a lovely voice.' I opened my bill to sing and dropped a fine piece of cheese. Fox walked away with my cheese and had the nerve to tell me that I sing out of tune."

Rabbit said, "I still have cramps from the sour grapes he traded for my sweet, ripe ones. He told me that sour grapes are full of vitamin C."

"I was picking chestnuts the other day," said Donkey. "Fox stopped by and offered to help me. When we were finished, he said, 'You are bigger than I am, so you should have the larger share.' He handed me the heavier sack. I carried it home, only to discover it was full of rocks."

Just then Bear appeared. He was very excited.

"You don't have to laugh at me anymore. I have
a beautiful tail, too," he announced.
"Who's laughing at you?" and "What tail?" asked
the animals.
Bear showed them Fox's note.
"Welcome to the club," Donkey said.
"What did he wheedle out of you?"
"My honey," said Bear.

"You might as well stick that note to your stump and wag it, because Fox will never part with his tail," said Rabbit.

"It's time we got even with Fox and taught him a lesson," said Crow.

"But how?" asked Bear.

"I think I know," said Crow. "Just keep reminding him his tail belongs to you."

"I'll go right now," said Bear.

"Wait," said Crow. "We'll all go. But tonight. Late."

It was midnight, and Fox was fast asleep in his
den. Suddenly there was a banging on the door.
"Who could it be at this time of night?" he wondered.

"It's me," called Bear. "I brought my friends to see
my tail."
"At this hour?" grumbled Fox. "Couldn't you wait
till morning?"

"It will only take a few minutes," said Bear.
"All right," said Fox. "Have a quick look and go.
I've got a lot of sleeping to do."

"Oh my," said Crow. "This poor tail looks terrible.
It needs to be taken care of at once."
"What do you know about fur, you featherbrain?"
said Fox, and slammed the door.

Bear and his friends all went to Bear's den
to plan their next move.

A few hours later, just before sunrise, Bear was back at Fox's den, this time alone.

"I came to groom my tail," he called.

"What?" said the sleepy Fox. "You can't just bother me any time you please."

"I didn't come to see you," said Bear. "I came to take care of my tail. Let me in."

"Okay, okay," said Fox. "But whatever it is that you want to do, please do it quickly."

Bear wasted no time. He placed Fox
on a stool and went to work.

All during the washing, squeezing, and combing, Bear
described other plans he had for his tail.

"I'll curl it and dye it pink, then decorate it with ribbons and hair clips. In the fall, I might even shave it and use the hair to make a pillow for my winter sleep."

"No, you won't," said Fox, jumping off the stool.
"Here, take your honey back. The deal is off."

"No, it's not," said Bear. "Only a fool would trade
such a splendid tail for a half-empty jar of honey."
"What else do you want?" asked the stunned Fox.
Bear said, "I'll have the honey, but in addition I
want some fine cheese, a bag of chestnuts, and
some sweet, ripe grapes."
"That is ridiculous," screamed Fox.
"Then I want my tail now," said Bear.

"Very well," said Fox. "I'll give the tail to you, but I'll have to ask you to wait outside. This is a serious operation."

"I'll give you ten minutes," said Bear. "But don't try any tricks."
Bear waited patiently outside, when suddenly he heard screams of pain coming through the door.

A few minutes later, Fox limped out, a huge towel
wrapped around his waist. In his hand he held a tail.
"You really cut it off?" said the horrified Bear.
"Isn't that what you wanted?" asked Fox.
"Yes," said Bear. "But it looks awful, like an old broom."
"Well, that's what happens to a chopped-off tail," said
Fox, and he threw it at Bear's feet.

Just as Fox turned to go back in, the towel
came undone, and his real tail sprang out.
"You liar," shouted Bear "It <u>is</u> a broom."
He grabbed Fox by his real tail.

"Please let go," begged Fox. "I was only joking.
I'll give you everything you asked for, and I'll even
let you wear my tail. But only once," he added.

Down by the stream, Bear's friends were waiting and wondering what was keeping Bear. He finally showed up, sporting a handsome foxtail.

"He actually gave you his tail," said the astonished Crow.

"And everything else he took from us," said Bear.

"How did you do it?" asked Rabbit.

"With your help," said Bear. "Now let's all have a picnic."

"Perhaps we should have invited Fox," said Donkey.

"No need," said Bear.

He took off his jacket—and there was Fox.

But Fox slipped off Bear's back and, without saying a word, slunk away, never to be seen again, at least not in that part of the forest.